For Ever
– S.Y.B.

The author would like to acknowledge the invaluable assistance of *Around the Roman Table* by Patrick Faas; *Cookery and Dining in Imperial Rome*, by Apicius, and translated by Joseph Dommers Vehling; and *A Day in the Life of Ancient Rome*, by Alberto Angela, in the writing of this book.

To my husband, Jake, who will eat anything, and I admire that.
– F.L.

Text © 2022 Shirin Yim Bridges
Illustrations © 2022 Fiona Lee

Book design by Melissa Nelson Greenberg & Regina Shklovsky

Published in 2022 by CAMERON + COMPANY, a division of ABRAMS.

Library of Congress Cataloging-in-Publication Data available.
ISBN: 978-1-951836-48-1

Printed in China

10 9 8 7 6 5 4 3 2 1

CAMERON KIDS is an imprint of CAMERON + COMPANY

CAMERON + COMPANY
Petaluma, California
www.cameronbooks.com

EAT YOUR PEAS, JULIUS!

Even Caesar Must Clean His Plate

Shirin Yim Bridges

Fiona Lee

cameron kids

Time's up, little Julius,
put your game away.
Your dad's having a banquet;
you've a new role to play.

For the first time this evening,
you'll have your own seat—
or rather a couch,
as men lie down to eat.

First, your toga praetexta;
please hold still if you can.
Over left arm, under right arm . . .
See? You're almost a man.

Clean your hands in rose water
so they're fragrant and sweet.
Let them take off your sandals
and wash your wee feet.

Oh! Here come the oysters
paraded in on their shells,
amidst a sea of smoked whole fish—
how delightful that smells!

Not tempting? Maybe something from the selection of fowl? Peacocks, parrots, flamingos—but we're fresh out of owls.

No fowl for you, Julius?
You really must eat!
Have some stuffed sow's udders
or some boiled camel's feet!

Here's a plate of sea scorpions—
a sweet custard with fish—
pig lungs stuffed with fresh figs—
veggies and brains in one dish!

By Jove, sweet Julius,
how you fuss about food!
A little baked dormouse
is a treat—don't be rude!

You should realize you're fortunate
to have rodents at all.
There are children without food
in Cisalpine Gaul!

Very well, little Caesar,
because you said "please,"
you're excused from the table—
but first, EAT YOUR PEAS!!!

Julius Caesar grew up to be a Roman general. But he started off as a little kid
who had to clean his plate every night—just like you!

Many people think that Julius Caesar grew up to be a Roman emperor—but he did not. He was at one point the most powerful man in ancient Rome, but his adopted son, Octavian, became Caesar Augustus, Rome's first emperor.

Kids growing up like Julius in ancient Rome had a lot of toys that we still play with today: bats and balls, kites, and toy swords. They also had a version of checkers called *ludus latrunculorum*, which was a war game like our modern chess.

Although children and sometimes women sat in chairs or stood to eat, men lay down on couches or beds called *kline*. Dining rooms in wealthier homes usually had three couches gathered around one central table. The lower classes often did not have dining rooms or kitchens at all. Many Romans got all their meals from take-out restaurants called *thermopolia*.

As a high-born Roman boy, Julius Caesar would have worn the toga praetexta on special occasions, when he had to behave like a grown-up. His toga would have differed from the toga virilis that his father wore by having a broad purple band around its edge. Putting on a toga was so complicated that both Julius and his father would have needed help.

Every Roman banquet began with all the diners being brought water with which to wash their hands, and then having their dusty sandals removed and their feet washed.

Eating seafood was very popular, even though Rome was a seven-hour walk from the closest port. Imagine how that seafood must have smelled! Although ancient Romans did have ice, it's usually mentioned as being used for keeping wine and water cold, not fish!

Romans also liked to eat birds. In addition to the chickens, ducks, and geese we're familiar with, they ate parrots, flamingos, ostriches, cranes, thrushes, doves, and songbirds like nightingales. Peacock tongues were a special delicacy.

How do we know what the ancient Romans ate? The descriptions of particular banquets have survived, as has a collection of recipes called *The Book of Apicius.* And we can tell many details of ancient Roman life from the ruins of Pompeii as well as the remains of Roman toilets. Analyzing the remains of Roman poop can tell us what they ate!

Baked dormouse was a particular Roman favorite, so much so that special dormouse-fattening jars were invented.

There were hungry children all over the vast territories of the Roman Republic, even in Rome itself! Julius Caesar, being from a wealthy family, never had to worry about his food. But to his credit, he never became a glutton either. When he grew up and became one of the most powerful men in history, he still ate very simply.

Although Julius came from a well-off family, they were not particularly famous or powerful. Nobody could have guessed that Julius would grow up to become such a powerful statesman—so powerful that he set the model for all the following Roman rulers, who called themselves emperors. *Caesar* came to mean "powerful ruler."